A POCKET OF PEBBLES

8 ROMANTIC SHORT STORIES

CATHERINE EVANS

CONTENTS

COPYRIGHT

ISBN (print): 978-0-6485314-0-1
ISBN-13: 978-0-6485314-0-1

This is a collection of 8 romantic short stories, all mentioning gemstones. They were written for the Romance Writers of Australia's annual short story contest between 2008 and 2014. Each story is a tiny pebble—less than 3000 words.

There are no connections between the stories, except for a touch of romance.

You may find birds and vampires, cops and crashes, married couples and young love. Some are serious, some amusing, some crazy madness.

I hope you may find a story that suits you.

Watery Liaisons: Life-long friends, Eloise and Daniel, have recently become lovers with accidental consequences. Will this ruin their connection?

An Old-Fashioned Courtship: A colourful love story with a difference.

From Disaster Comes Love: Samantha sits on the train next to the man who's held her attention for weeks. When the train crashes, will they lose each other?

'Twas the Night before Conference: Unpublished paranormal romance writer, Juliette, sees a gorgeous man when others see thin air. Eris is an emotional vampire. Is she his human mate, or victim?

Last Hope Safari: Married couple, Matilda and

Jake, want a child but years of failing has fractured them. Jake hopes for natural healing, but is it too late?

Diamond Shield: Policewoman, Kendra, goes undercover at a speed dating night. After the operation is successful, she meets Mitch; not the gorgeous, witty date but part of the job. Will they mix business and pleasure?

Farewell Sapphire: Two years ago, Darren promised to come back for Sapphire. Today's her eighteenth birthday, dare she hope he keeps the promise?

Moonstone Madness: Kat wins a race horse at the picnic races, but she'd prefer to win the heart of the horse trainer, Josh. Can she be that lucky?

ACKNOWLEDGMENTS

~

A huge thank you to the Romance Writers of Australia for holding the Little Gems short story contest, to Lis for managing this every year which is a huge task, and to all the readers who have judged it.

The short story contest is for members, and each year a different, nominated gemstone must be included. The stories can be no longer than 3000 words and must be a romance suitable for all.

I've entered this contest for some years, with one entry (Diamond Shield) making the annually published anthology for the top 12-16 stories (it placed second).

The gemstones for each year were: 2009 Turquoise; 2010 Topaz; 2011 Garnet; 2012 Diamond; 2013 Sapphire; 2014 Moonstone.

I've had quite a few wonderful critique partners who have worked on some/all of these stories. Many thanks to Mervet, Sandra, Judy, Anita Joy, Pam, Lisa Ireland, Ainslie Paton and Jennie Jones for their assistance.

Much thanks to my family and friends for their support, especially my husband.

Thank you, Readers. I've collected these stories together in the hope that you might enjoy them. Without you, these would sit on my computer doing nothing but chewing up space.

Cath xo

WATERY LIAISONS

*D*aniel McClosker sliced through the water, his body creating a wake behind him. His powerful shoulders were lifted above the water, muscles gleaming, as his arms rolled up and over, hands slicing cleanly into the glistening blue. His head rolled rhythmically from left to right with every alternate stroke, breathing the chilly air into his lungs to feed the muscles and continue his powerful swim.

Is there a name for a man you sleep with too often to be called a one-night stand but you don't spend enough time with to be called a lover?

I'd known Daniel since we were, I don't know, maybe three years old. We took swimming lessons together, or so our mothers' tell us. We don't remember meeting, we just remember rarely being apart. He runs the local swimming pool in summer and teaches life saving and resuscitation in winter. I teach swimming in summer at his pool, and I've just finished teacher training. I'll be teaching at the local primary school in February.

Last night my well-planned life came to a halt. Now my life's more like Daniel's—unplanned, 'a discovery every day' as he calls it. I don't like it. In fact, I'm terrified.

I look a mess. My eyes are bloodshot, standing out from my face. I didn't even brush my hair and I know instead of sitting flat against my head in a pixie cut, or gelled up spiky in my mad pixie do, it's every which way—flat, standing up, squished, matted. I'd managed to drag on swimmers and grab my towel. I wanted to swim a few laps and try to work some sense into my brain before I have to speak to Daniel.

Daniel gave me the pool gate key years ago, so I could swim with him in the peace of the early hours before patrons filled the pool. It's our time. Not that we speak. We just lap together, well, not together. What I should say is, we swim together. Daniel swims much faster than I do. It's our special time. I have to hold that thought close. It's going to stop me drowning this morning.

I slide into the cool crisp water, feeling it lap against my body. I breathe out a deep soulful sigh as I slip beneath, knowing that it's just made my hair respectable; although my eyes will take some time! I stretch myself upwards and take a deep breath as I surface. I push back towards the edge of the pool, curl my legs beneath me and push off. The water sluices over me. Each part of my body feels the cool touch and responds with a shiver of goose bumps. My body propels me underwater for a while and then I arch my back until I surface. I lift my arms in the familiar freestyle crawl. My feet kick out the familiar rhythm. My mind goes blank as I follow the black line and push myself forwards to the other end of the pool.

No matter how many times the water caresses my body,

it never consumes me like Daniel's hand. I feel the goose bumps cover my skin as I slide into the water but they are never the hot goose bumps that Daniel's touch produces. When I stretch my body into the water, and feel it slide against me caressing every pore; it's not like Daniel's body stretching out against mine covering me from head to toe. The water is like a soothing, soft massage. Daniel is like white-hot iron.

Each stroke I ask myself how to tell Daniel. I replay scenarios in my mind but they play the same as last night. Hopeless. How do you tell someone that together you've made a huge mistake? How do you tell them the mistake is yours to live with and they can leave, without making a judgment or implying that you don't want them?

I was so concerned with my thoughts that I swam smack into Daniel as he stood against the far wall. My head ploughed into his stomach as my hand slid down his leg. The frisson of goose bumps was there, even in the water, almost heating the water touching me. I stood up in front of him.

"You look like hell." His voice growled; the tone so much deeper than his normal voice.

I frowned as I looked up at him. Concern, fear, confusion, and sheer happiness at seeing him coursed through my body. I felt my nipples pucker, my skin tighten and my face crease into half a smile. My normal body reactions to Daniel.

"Thank you, and good morning to you too, Daniel. What's wrong?"

"I should be asking you that question."

He stroked my cheek gently with his finger tips sliding

over my cheek to my jaw where his fingers traced along to my chin. It was heaven. Water droplets could trace the same path without me even knowing. Daniel's fingertips were no heavier than water droplets, yet I felt the pathway as if he had run a burning stick along.

I leaned closer to him and he dragged me against his body. He stood with his back against the blocks, his legs stretched forward and slightly bent so that he was almost as short as I. My body slid against his, my legs between his, my torso against his, the tips of my nipples grazing his chest when it rose on each breath. He was breathing hard after his swim. I half hoped that his breathing would become normal quickly. I couldn't think when my nipples grazed his chest, even through my swimming costume.

"The mothers were talking about you last night. Your mother said you were dreadfully upset. She thought my mother might know why. What upset you, Sunshine?"

I bit my lip and looked up at his face. A face so familiar to me that I knew he was concerned by the look in his deep green eyes, the subtle pout of his lips and the set of his jaw. What should I say to him?

"Dan, I'm in trouble," I whispered as the tears welled in my eyes. I choked them back. I will not cry again.

"What? Tell me what's wrong. How much trouble? We'll fix it."

"It's going to affect you too Dan. And I'm so sorry. I'm so sorry." I crumpled against his chest, my forehead lying in the hollow between his chest and stomach. I could hear his heart pounding. It was soothing, as were his hands that wrapped around me and stroked my back.

"Have you found a man and you're leaving me?" Daniel asked softly.

I could feel the rumble in his chest as he spoke. Was that his deepest fear? A tiny glimmer of hope sparkled in my heart, like a glistening droplet of water hanging from the tip of a leaf after rain. So fragile, the slightest change of breeze could send it freefalling. I took a deep breath and held it tight as I looked up to his face.

His face was tight, tense, lined with worry. His eyes refused to look at me but drifted off to the horizon as if distancing himself from me. His body still held me close, although there seemed to be water slipping between us where I was sure there hadn't been any before.

"I'm pregnant," I said, trying desperately to keep my voice steady because I knew each time I'd practiced saying it, my voice cracked on the last word.

His head snapped down to search my face. His eyes drilled into mine, searching for something that I wasn't sure he'd find. His hands crushed me to him. No longer soothing, but claiming me—or maybe that's just my fanciful imagination.

"To who?" he asked as his eyes held mine in an icy glare.

I smacked my curled fist against his side, frustrated that he had to ask me that question. I had been with others in the past but they paled with comparison to Daniel. This summer was the first time we'd taken our relationship beyond an easy friendship. The past eight weeks we'd had ... what would you call it? ... a steamy affair, torrid encounters, wild passionate sex. We'd never talked about it or given it a name.

It started out one morning. We'd been swimming and we stopped to talk about, who knew, I certainly can't remember. Our eyes locked, our mouths kept talking, my foot touched his leg as I tread water, his hand grasped my ankle, our mouths stopped talking and slammed together in a kiss of fire and passion. We never even made it out of the pool. We'd had sex there. My swimmers grasped in his hand, his around his ankles. My legs around his hips, the water holding me. It was fast and urgent. No words spoken, just our bodies meeting, in need, hunger and passion. It had probably been brewing since we were teenagers. Who knew?

"You," I muttered. "You, Dan. All the sex we've had each morning, in the pool, without thinking about anything at all." I punched his shoulders repeatedly as he held me, frustration welling up inside me. I was screaming inside but kept my voice low. "Goddamn, I know better than this. I never even thought of anything. Contraception never crossed my mind. Why? Why, Dan?" A sob was wrenched from deep inside me but I wouldn't cry again.

Daniel cradled me, his huge chest my pillow, his chin against the top of my head. I felt secure and safe for the first time in the last twelve hours. I had hoped Daniel would protect me and our unborn child.

'I'm glad you told me, Sunshine," he eventually said. "I have to open the pool. Can you come back here tonight and we'll work something out?"

Each word slammed against me until I felt like I was dumped at sea. My heart sank. This was one of the outcomes I feared. Not the worst. That was to be abandoned completely and for Daniel to deny paternity. So

I wasn't at the bottom of despair. I was a rung higher than that.

"Work something out?" I stammered, my voice threadbare and devoid of feeling.

"Sunshine, I'm always here for you. Of course I'll be with you now. You've had twelve hours to think. Please give me that at least."

Daniel's voice begged. My head told me he was right. I had to give him some time. I'd known for almost a day, so I owed him at least twelve hours. I nodded and prised myself from his body, feeling like an oyster ripped from my post.

I left the pool and spent the day alone. I wondered if anyone noticed that I was hollow. I went through the motions of living but I wasn't alive. I wondered of the small life inside me knew how I felt. Would it also cease to live?

I knew falling in love with Daniel was stupid. It had never been a conscious decision. I don't know when I fell in love with him. I don't know that I could have stopped it happening. Daniel was always there. The physical nature of our relationship these past few weeks was just ... stupid ... but in a way, an inevitable change, a natural progression.

My phone alarm beeped at seven p.m. The pool closed then. I showered and tried to find something to wear. What do you wear to a meeting that would decide your fate? Casual? Conservative? Funeral clothes? Funeral clothes seemed appropriate but... he'd said "...come back here...". Did that mean the pool—in the pool?

I made the decision that I would indeed wear swimmers and stand where I'd stood this morning. If that wasn't what Daniel McClosker wanted, then too bad! I pulled on my bright blue bikini. Not the sort of swimmers I wore to swim laps, or teach lessons. The bikini was for pleasure. It matched my eyes.

I let myself into the pool. It was silent. The far end, dark. The closer end glistened in the fading sunlight. I headed towards the far end. As I got closer, I noticed an air mattress drifting on the water, a basket on top caused it to dip slightly in the middle. And then I saw Daniel behind it, almost submerged in the water. My heart made a tiny skip, a symbol of hope that I quickly squashed. *Don't hope and you won't be shattered.*

I dropped my bag and towel on the grandstand seats before I slipped silently into the water, submerging and swimming beneath until I was alongside Daniel. I was torn between surfacing next to him or sliding along his body to surface, but body contact was too overly friendly and I wasn't feeling quite that nice.

I popped up beside him like a seal emerging from the ocean. He turned to look at me and smiled; genuinely smiled, as if he was happy to see me. I felt my traitorous heart flutter again in hope.

His green eyes danced as the setting sun threw sunbeams across the water towards us. If I hadn't been feeling so miserable, I would have been dazzled by the sunset and how it framed Daniel's face.

"I've thought about you all day," Daniel admitted as he reached his hands to cradle my face and press a soft kiss against my lips.

I responded to his kiss, how could I not? His lips were full and beautiful. Tonight they were soft and drugging, eliciting soft moans from me as they nibbled against my harder lips, pulling them out of the harsh line they had been stuck in all day. His lips coaxed mine open until his tongue could slip inside and hypnotise me under his spell.

My legs had wrapped around his hips. My hands clung to his shoulders, or curled behind his neck, seeming to move of their own accord. My body betrayed my mind. I didn't want to feel loved and safe in his arms if he was going to abandon me. I mentally cursed my traitorous body.

He slid his mouth from mine, slowly, and nibbled his way along my jaw to the soft skin beneath my earlobe. I shuddered in delight, responding again. He licked behind my ear and breathed softly. Another delicious shudder rippled through my body and into the surrounding water.

"Eloise, you are the sunshine in my life."

I heard the words murmured against my ear. I felt his lips dance across the sensitive skin on the shell of my ear as he spoke. I know the words permeated my brain. I just couldn't understand them. They made no sense to me.

"I am never happier than when I'm with you."

Again, I could hear, feel, and this time even understand the words, but still I didn't believe them.

"I wish I'd told you this before this morning."

I moved slightly. This wasn't what I'd imagined. There was something happening that I couldn't comprehend. I pulled my head back to look at his face.

His face was exquisite. Bathed in dying sunbeams, which gave an intensity to the strong lines I'd loved through my life. His green eyes burned with a seriousness I'd never seen. His lips formed serious words that I'd never believed I would ever hear.

"Eloise Carter, you are the love of my life. Would you consider marrying me ... please?"

Astonished, my mouth fell open. He moved his hand in front of my face and a tiny green box sat in the palm of his hand. I stared at the box; back to his face; the box; his face. What was I to do? Did I have to say something? What had he just asked me?

A cloud vanished from inside my head and the hardness lifted from my heart. I stared into the depths of his green eyes and I knew he was honestly asking me to be his wife. My chest of hopes sprang open and sang in my heart.

I licked my lips and dragged my voice from the depths of my heart, "Daniel," was all I could manage. I kissed him, or he kissed me. It didn't matter, we were kissing, the small box pressed against my shoulder blades as a reminder of his love.

We pulled apart reluctantly as air became necessary. He again held the box out before my face.

"I bought you a ring. I hope you like it."

Daniel's voice was hesitant, nervous almost. It surprised me. I'd always known the confident Daniel. This was a new side to him. Imagine, a new side to him after knowing him forever.

"Did you buy this today?" I asked him as I lifted the lid on the box, regretting the marks that my wet hands left.

"No," he replied reluctantly. "I bought it weeks ago and have stupidly been too scared to ask you."

That stunned me into silence. Weeks ago? Weeks ago? He had known he wanted to marry me before I even knew that I did? The last twenty four hours of agony had been for nothing? I had doubted him for nought?

I opened the box to find the most beautiful ring I'd ever imagined. In a platinum setting lay a pear cut diamond surrounded on each side by oval turquoise gemstones. The diamond dazzled and the turquoise lay warm and protective either side. I gasped; stunned that Daniel would buy such an exquisitely beautiful ring.

"How did you find this?" I asked breathlessly.

"I designed it myself. I wanted a stunning diamond, because diamonds are forever. The turquoise stones match your eyes and are for strength, good fortune and protection. I thought they needed to be on both sides to protect both of us forever. Do you like it?" he asked and I nodded in response, speechless.

I took the ring from the box and held it out to him, my left hand dangling so he could slide the ring into place.

As Daniel took my hand and kissed each finger tip before he slid the exquisite ring into place, I watched the last rays of sunlight dance across his face before they brought sparkles shooting from my diamond.

My heart soared and my mouth finally uttered the words that had lodged in my throat earlier. "Oh, Daniel. I love you so much. Yes. I'll marry you."

 The End

AN OLD-FASHIONED COURTSHIP

I saw him across the expanse of garden and my world changed. He was sitting, not a care in the world, enjoying the sunshine. My heart stopped beating. It was as if the world had turned sepia and he alone remained coloured. He was stunning. *Magnifique.*

I didn't have the courage to go up to him, although I wanted to. The girls around me must have noticed my gaze because a cacophony of sound erupted around me and I watched his head turn my way. I blushed. My blush was but a faded reflection of the colour of his chest. His chest was covered in the most magnificent fire engine red. Stunning.

He came towards me. No, he didn't just come towards me, he zeroed in on me, as if we were the only beings in the entire world. I could tell by looking at him that he had great confidence. He didn't wear anything but the brightest colours to ensure he was noticed. Oh, he took my breath away. I'll try to describe his colour sense but I know it will sound awful, just please believe me when I say that it was arrestingly beautiful.

The fire engine red covered his chest and drew your eye to the muscles beneath. He was strong, I could tell. As he neared me, I thought I could detect the beating of his heart beneath but I may be just fanciful.

Emerald green covered his back and upper limbs, with dollops of lime. A coat of emerald. It should have clashed with the brightest red, instead it set it off. The darker coloured coat focussed your attention on his chest. But I noticed the strength hidden by this emerald coat. I noticed and dreamed of being beneath those limbs, snuggled against his chest, safe from the sepia world. I took a quick gulp of air as I continued my evaluation, as I knew he was doing to me.

His lower limbs should have made me laugh but again, the confidence it takes to wear such outlandish colours together had me astounded and in awe. Navy and brilliant turquoise adorned his lower body. I couldn't even call them stripes. It was slashes of the most stunningly brilliant turquoise that flashed as he moved. How it was interspersed with the navy I'll never know. It took my breath away.

He stood before me in his splendid confidence and dipped his head respectfully. He asked me to join him in a walk around the garden. I was suddenly shy, embarrassed even. How could I, dowdy as I am and lacking in the confidence that he so obviously owned, be seen accompanying him? The girls around me twittered and gasped but my best-friend nudged me and I regained my manners quickly.

"Of course. It would be my absolute pleasure," I stuttered and stammered, blushing deeper as I did so.

We took a tour of the gardens. They were beautiful and any other day I would have been mesmerised by the natural beauty of the flowers, trees, shrubs and herbs. Today, it paled beside my companion. He became my world.

"I've noticed you around," he told me coyly, as I blushed in response. "I'm incredibly attracted to you."

"To me?" I managed to blurt out in my breathless shock.

He nodded that beautiful face of his and brought it close against mine. The breath left my body as he slid his cheek slowly against mine. It was the most arousing touch, yet, hardly a touch. I almost fainted then and there.

"Would you care to spend time with me?"

He was so polite, well-educated, exquisite in every way. I was completely unprepared for the sudden interest from him. I wished I had have seen him notice me before so I could at least have prepared for this onslaught of emotion.

I agreed to spend time with him. It could hardly hurt my standing in the community to be seen stepping out with such a handsome fellow, even if it didn't last. I have so little confidence or optimism. I was completely taken aback by his interest in me. There were many others more beautiful and outgoing than I. I was rendered almost speechless in his company. How could he have liked me at all?

I rushed home, as soon as I could politely leave him, to talk to my mother. I knew she would have some sage advice.

"How wonderful for you, Angel," she exclaimed as I told her of my morning. "He is very well thought of, from a good family and I doubt you could find a better partner. You would produce wonderful children."

I was shocked. Obviously my mother had been well-prepared for this event. Why had she not prepared me for it? Why was I so taken aback?

"Mother, how can you speak of grandchildren? I'm not

ready. I'm not even ready for a partner, let alone one so incredible."

"Sweetheart, you will be. Just spend time with him and you'll see." She smiled that secretive mother-smile that you know means that they know far more than you and are secretly just waiting to say "I told you so". It's not unpleasant, but can be a little annoying.

I spent time with him. That's probably an understatement. Every waking moment of my life over the next week was spent in his company. It became that I couldn't breathe without his stunning beauty being inhaled along with the required air.

I ate with him. He took me to beautiful places to eat. Much further than I had been before. I think he took me away from our community so that he could be alone with me. And after the first time, when I was too nervous to appreciate it, I found I loved being alone with him. I enjoyed his company. He knew places that I had never seen before and he seemed to appreciate the same beauty in our surroundings that I could see. He loved flowers and would spend many hours in some of my favourite gardens while I exclaimed over the new flowers he found tucked in hideaway places. Or else he showed me new flowers in new places, some with colours and perfumes I'd never dreamed were possible. It was a wonderful time.

I realised that my mother was right. The longer I spent with him, the more I wanted to spend the rest of my life with him. His touches set my heart fluttering. He need only move his head a certain way and my stomach tensed in expectation of his whisper soft caress. Not yet a kiss, but I was waiting for that special moment. Actually, to tell you the truth, I was almost ready to make the move myself. I was so ready for his kiss.

One day he took me way up to the highest point around. I'd never been this high before and the view was spectacular. We could see over the treetops and down onto the valley where my friends and family lived. I felt aglow just looking at the vista laid out before me.

He snuggled close to me and I thought my heart would beat right out of my chest.

"I adore you," he said simply.

I looked at him and tried to put all my feelings into that gaze so it could tell him I adored him and so much more. The things that I could never find words to convey.

He must have read the exact message for he turned his head in that peculiar way he has and nuzzled my cheek before turning towards me and feathering me with a kiss that scorched me to the extremities of my body. I was branded 'his' by that kiss. Never would I see anyone else but him.

"I'd like you to be my life partner. Would you do me the honour of accepting my offer?"

"Oh, yes," I breathed in a raspy, husky voice, before sealing my fate with another divine kiss.

He stood up and celebrated by calling in his loudest voice, a note of such shrill exuberance and happiness that I couldn't help but join in. The sound of our delight brought our friends and family to investigate. I beamed with ecstatic joy as he told them of our decision. It was a magnificent occasion.

My mother and father radiated with pride. My sisters glowed with envy, but also happiness for me. My friends strutted, distressed that I had found the first mate, but trying desperately to find their own. I had started the commitment contagion and all wanted to be the next infected.

I sat next to him, feeling his warmth surround me, almost bursting with happiness. I saw my life ahead of me, filled with my fantastic partner and our glorious children. Life was wonderful.

Noise from children below startled me from my thoughts. Their laughter and voices drifted towards me on the warm currents of air that rose from the heated earth into the cooler leafiness of the trees. Their voices were shrill with wonder and their words made me laugh.

"Hey, look at all those King Parrots," one child called out to the others.

"Oh yeah, weird."

"How many do you reckon there are?"

"Looks like hundreds."

"It looks like they're having a party."

The children rode off on their bicycles to new adventures, their laughter trailing on the currents behind them.

They were right. We were having a party... my engagement party.

The End

FROM DISASTER COMES LOVE

I ran down the stairs, leapt onto the train just as the doors were closing, and sighed with relief. *I'd made it.* Nothing had gone right today. It had been one disaster after another—I overslept, spilt my coffee, was late for work, my lunch fell on the floor and my big new deal fell through.

I looked up to see if there was a seat and there he was, Mr Turquoise Eyes, smiling at me an empty seat beside him. My heart, which was already pounding from my run to make the train, thumped harder. I sat beside him. *Maybe my day had just improved.*

"I didn't think you'd make it," he said as I sat down. His voice was a purr in my ear.

I was panting and not only because of the effect he was having on me. "Me too," I gasped as I tried to catch my breath.

My breath slowed and I sank back against the seat. As I relaxed and inhaled, I was suddenly aware of his hard thigh pressed against mine. His hip touching my hip, his arm my elbow, his shoulder my shoulder. The left side of my body zinged. *What was I going to say to him?*

"I've seen you on the train for weeks. I can't believe I've sat next to you." The words left my mouth before my brain censored them. *What an idiot!* I closed my eyes and scrunched my face, wishing the words could dissolve in the air before he heard them. No such luck. His chuckle sizzled its way down my spine until I squirmed in my seat. Now that wasn't a good idea either. I just felt his body more and that certainly was not going to help my brain form coherent thoughts, let alone words!

There was silence. I expected nothing else. I shook my head in misery. I'd just made a total fool of myself, there was no way he'd speak to me now. The silence became suffocating. I wanted to jump up and run to another carriage but I thought that would only make me appear more idiotic—if that was at all possible.

"I didn't know you'd even seen me," he almost whispered against my ear; his head had turned towards me. I felt his light breath on the fine hairs, just beneath my ear on the point of my jaw. My face burned as the fine hairs danced in the breath.

"Oh, I've seen you. From the first day I caught this train. My old train trips used to be so boring but since moving here, I've enjoyed them." I rolled my eyes and wondered how my mouth had become totally dislocated from my brain. I had turned into a crazy girl. Next I'd be telling him I wanted to jump his body.

"You moved when?" he asked.

We both paused and then in unison said, "Seventeenth of August," and laughed at each other.

There was no pretence now. We were no longer sitting facing forward and speaking as if we weren't speaking. We had turned our bodies towards each other. His foot touched my foot. His knee touched my knee. His hips had moved from my side. They no longer touched mine but supported his body so it was almost opposite mine. His head and mine were turned so that we looked directly at each other. It was all-consuming. I felt special, as if I was cocooned in his body, like a membrane surrounded us and kept us from the outside world. As if the world stood still to allow us the time to speak these first important words.

His face was perfect. His eyes a clear blue, almost turquoise. His blonde-brown hair fell in caresses against the sides of his face and across his brow. His lips were full, strong and pouty in a way that begged to be kissed. His jaw was strong and square, like a pedestal holding his face high to best display the beauty above.

"Where did you move from?" he asked as the train shuddered and jerked, throwing us against one another. Our hands touched as we steadied each other.

I opened my mouth to speak but the train became a percussion of sound—crashing, grinding, rumbling, screeching and then the clash of kettle drum and cymbal. We were thrown against each other as the train reared, suspended in mid air for a moment before crashing to the ground spewing passengers from their seats.

For a few moments it was chaos in silence. Ridiculously, I felt safe.

And then the silence was broken by metal screaming against metal. As that subsided, the ear splitting sound of humans in panic began. Blood curdling screams, deep moans, ear piercing shrieks, rumbling moans of abject pain.

My eyes were clenched shut. I was silent and so was he. I could feel him though. His body was wrapped around me, his heart beat strongly against mine. His arms encircled my waist. My arms around his shoulders. My face pressed into the hollow beneath his collarbone. I was protected and secure amid the horror around me. The membrane surrounded us still.

I turned my lips to the base of his throat, that dip between collarbones. I slid my tongue against his flesh there, feeling his pulse beneath the skin. I could tell when he felt my heated, wet touch as his pulse quickened. "Are you okay?" I asked as I felt the pulse rate lift.

"No," he replied thickly, his voice against my ear.

I tensed in his arms. *Please don't let me lose him when I've just found him.* "What's wrong? What can I do?"

His teeth nipped at the top of my ear and caused me to jump beneath him, well, as much as you can jump when you are crushed by a man. "Stop teasing me when we're lucky to be alive," he ground between his teeth. I tried to smother a giggle as he continued, "I can't walk out of here with... you know... everything at attention."

I couldn't help myself, I started to laugh. I felt it rumble from deep within my stomach and gurgle through my body before hissing through my lungs and erupting from my mouth. It wasn't the place for laughter but I couldn't help it. I was in love with Mr Turquoise Eyes and he seemed to at least like me.

I slid my hands into his hair and massaged his scalp. If I wasn't pinned beneath him I would be tasting his lips right now, but that wasn't possible. I couldn't move beneath him. I slid my hands from his hair down his back. I traced the strength of his large, muscled shoulders, and down over his shoulder blades. I skimmed the middle of his back, feeling the knobbly protrusions of his spine. Against his shirt lay a huge quantity of dust, glass, metal and rubbish. I could feel no injury. I was relieved.

I cracked open my eyes to face reality. The train carriage was a wreck. What had been clear air was now turbid dust particles. The lights were extinguished so only muted evening sunlight made it through the thick dusty air.

I lifted my now bare feet and slid them along his legs, feeling only dust and glass – no blood, no protrusions, no damage, just hard muscle beneath his chinos. He groaned beneath me.

"Will you quit it," he growled in my ear. I stretched my legs against his again and lay almost still beneath him. I could feel the problem he had, it was pressed rigid against my thigh and I wanted more than to be lying immobile beneath him. Besides, his weight was starting to press against my chest and combined with the dusty air, I was having problems breathing.

"Where are your shoes?" he asked suddenly. I had no idea where my shoes were. They were only thongs, fancy thongs, but they had been lost when we fell. "How can we get out of here when you have no shoes?"

"My feet are tough. I usually wear no shoes."

"Let's try to move. Slowly." He rolled to the side, allowing me to wriggle against him but that only brought a growl and an admonition from him. We struggled upright and stood. We helped others who weren't badly injured to their feet. Emergency personnel came to assist. We were lucky; carriages further up were in a worse state than ours. An explosion had decimated the front carriage. The next two carriages had careened into the first. Our carriage had only come off the rails.

He stepped from the carriage, turned and held his arms out for me. He had such strong arms, large hands, a firm chest. Without question, I slid into his arms and he carried me gently but tightly. I was cushioned against his solid chest and it felt fantastic. I could feel the thud of his heart beat against my breast. One arm slid beneath my legs and my skin tingled through the light skirt I wore. His hand curled around my outer thigh and my skin burned there. His other arm supported my back and I have never felt safer. I know, it's ridiculous. Amid all this carnage and devastation, I could only think of Mr Turquoise Eyes and myself. Nothing mattered but my feelings for him. I was selfish, I know, but I had waited months to speak with him, and not even an explosion and train crash was going to steal this moment from me.

Once off the train, we were examined by medical staff, which meant I had to leave his arms, and ushered away from the site. We sat, our hands joined, with other uninjured passengers; none of us sure what to do next. We were all covered in dust, resembling nothing like the preened people who had boarded the train. Someone addressed our crowd, asked us to record our details with him before we left. We were then free to leave the disaster site.

My head was a foggy mess of blurred details and images, sound and silence, feelings and emotions. But when we were told we could leave, I panicked and my mind cleared. *I don't even know his name.* I looked at him in horror. It was all I could focus on.

He touched my face, gently cupping his hand around my jaw. "What's wrong?" he questioned me softly.

"I don't know your name," I blurted out, panic edging my voice sharply. "We could have died and I don't even know your name."

He smiled at me then, his turquoise eyes dancing in merriment, and whispered huskily against my ear, "And what a way to go, wrapped against you with a massive hard-on." I stared at him inanely and then I couldn't help myself, I burst out laughing. People turned to look at us, but I didn't care, the membrane was protecting us again. We leaned towards each other and our lips met. A first soft meeting of gentle proportions, a testing, tasting period. And then the emotion of the day took control and our kiss devoured each other. We crushed one another, lips parted, tongues duelling, teeth clashing. Energy and pent up adrenalin fuelled the kiss to an inferno. I was light-headed and clinging to him.

With destruction around us, it felt odd to be almost buoyant in mood. I suppose it was a reaction to surviving— we were alive, the world's sweeter—coupled with my reaction to Mr Turquoise Eyes—he was attracted to me, my bad day forgotten.

After some time we walked from the scene, hand in hand. He cleared his throat and stopped me beneath a large tree near a park. "I'm Dillon Clifton," he told me with a smile.

I was relieved to know his name. He was no longer a

fantasy, no longer Mr Turquoise Eyes. He was real and had a real name. I wanted to try it out and feel how it felt on my tongue. "Hi, Dillon Clifton," I said. His name filled my mouth. I could feel the name roll from my tongue to the roof of my mouth. It was lovely and rich. "I'm Samantha O'Collie, Sam."

It felt weird to be introducing ourselves after all we had already survived today. It seemed like an upside down relationship. Already he'd been wrapped around me, I had felt his reaction to my body, I had been snuggled in his arms, cradled against his chest, protected by him while we nearly died... and now we introduced ourselves. It was insane!

There was a long silence broken only by traffic going past. I could bear it no longer. "I don't want to be alone," I said in a whisper. I didn't want to walk away from him. I didn't want to be alone with the memories of what might have happened.

He coughed, almost apologetically, before he said, "If you stay with me, I'd want to finish what we started."

I gasped. I had fantasised about this man for weeks. Each day as he got off the train I longed to follow him. I felt bereft as the train pulled away from his station. Now, he was offering what I had been dreaming of. Was I brave enough to say 'yes'? I had never been so forward in a relationship. How could I even be contemplating staying with him and finishing what we started?

My stomach clenched in knots. I had to think fast. What was I to say? I could have died today. He could have died today. We may never have known each other's name. We may never have known we liked each other. Surely it was fate. My eyes searched his face in the twilight shadows.

His turquoise eyes were filled with longing and hope as they held mine.

"I'll stay with you." I answered. My voice was strong and firm. I had made my decision. Life was too short for hesitation.

~∞ The End ∞~

'TWAS THE NIGHT BEFORE CONFERENCE

*T*opaz eyes glittered in the semi-darkness of the hotel corridor. *Someone for the lift.* I held my hand against the lift doors, much to the amusement of the women sharing the lift. A striking man in a suit stepped from the shadows into the lift and politely nodded.

"Which floor?" I asked the girls, finger hovering over the panel.

I could just hear his response over the women tittering while they nudged one another. "It's already pushed, thanks."

"What?" I asked half-laughing, half-frowning. A little light-hearted teasing wasn't going to bother me. I was at my first Romance Writers of Australia Conference.

The air in the lift crackled, as if alive with electricity. There was something about a gathering of like-minded writers that sky-rocketed the energy levels.

I watched as the man glanced at the group and quickly looked away. His shoulders stiffened, spine stretched and then his shoulders flared while he breathed deeply.

Imagine sharing a lift with ten wound-up writing women!

He was probably early thirties. His long raven hair was tied with a leather strip and I guessed it would pass his shoulders when gloriously loose. A five o'clock shadow enhanced strong high cheekbones, a stage for those unusual eyes framed with thick, luscious lashes. He caught me studying him and I ducked my head.

I must have strange taste in men. None of the other girls seemed interested, yet I'm mesmerised ... purely as writing research.

The lift stopped at the fifth floor. On a roar of goodnights and promises for catching up at the next day's sessions, the lift emptied. Immediate silence. I was alone in the lift with the man. We breathed simultaneous sighs of relief, which made my lips twitch. I stifled a giggle.

I had to speak to him, to hear his voice. "You poor thing, fancy having to share a lift with all of us, when we're on such a high."

"It wasn't so bad." His voice was like heated honey; warm, thick, rich and delicious. It suited him, matched his eyes.

"Are you here for the conference or just here at the same time?" I wasn't sure if men attended the conference but I half-hoped this one did.

"I'm not part of the conference. What is it?"

Warmth crept from my jawline across my face. Do you tell a stranger when you're alone in a lift that you write romance? I opted for the safer option.

"A writers' conference."

A pause. "You're a writer?" His eyes flared and a small frown creased between his brows.

I don't consider myself a writer yet but I wasn't admitting that! "Not published yet but trying."

"What do you write?"

My stomach sank. Do I admit what I write? While making the decision the lift jerked then stopped at my floor. *I was saved.*

"This is my floor. It was nice speaking to you." The man held the doors for me as I had for him. A small butterfly took off in my stomach. Mimicking meant he was interested, didn't it?

Inhaling deeply as I walked past, I was overcome by the scent of musk and lavender, a strange mix for a man, although, for him entirely appropriate; relaxing and arousing.

I tried to memorise the moment. Commit it to words in my head for a story. I briefly closed my eyes blocking out the standard beige-with-a-splash-of-colour hotel corridor. His resonant voice broke the heavy silence. "So what *do* you write?"

He had followed me out. Of course! He had said the button was pushed.

"Ah, well, ah..." I hesitated not because I was embarrassed by what I wrote, just embarrassed to think that it sounded like a seduction.

"Don't be shy. I'm interested." His intense gaze was entrancing.

My lips spoke words before I'd decided what to say. "Paranormal romance."

A suspended moment. His glittering topaz gaze merged

with my sapphires. A long breath escaped his beautifully arched lips.

His question was barely a murmur across my nerve endings. "You write about mysterious, fantasy beings falling in love?" His tone was scathing disbelief.

Again my mouth and not brain answered. "Not with each other, with a human."

His comprehension was a breath that rippled across my face and neck. I tried to suppress the shiver. Warm honeyed cinnamon. I could smell it and taste it on my tongue.

"Why fantasy beings?" he asked.

His gaze dropped to my lips. I could feel them swelling to a pout. They became sensitive. I could feel each breath draw across my lips, stealing moisture as it raced through my mouth and down my throat.

I couldn't allow myself to be under some romantic spell. I struggled to drag my thoughts back to writing.

"Good question." And one I wasn't entirely sure how to answer. I ran my fingers across my scalp, lifting the hair that framed my face. I needed some time and cool air. "I find it easier to invent characters that aren't human but have human traits."

"What traits?"

I hooked my lower lip into my mouth. How do you explain about vampires wanting love more than blood? Or werewolves wanting a woman more than their pack? Or a giant ogre succumbing to a young fearless girl?

The man scratched his chin as he waited, his face creasing, ponderous.

"Their human weakness is found by only one woman."

He shifted his weight and fluttered his hand. *He wanted*

me to continue.

"They're the ultimate bad boy. Wild and wicked, they scare everyone... except their woman, their soul mate."

"And this is the human who sees them as they truly are?"

I nodded. I wasn't sure it was a question. I studied him. His tone was flat, indicating disinterest or disbelief, yet his eyes glowed with a ferocity that I can only associate with longing or passion. A strange reaction.

I was intrigued. I was being drawn closer to him, in proximity and mentally. I felt like I was in quicksand, sinking deeper with each word. And I was only confused, not terrified.

"Enough about me, what do you do?" I changed the focus to him, hoping to regain my senses.

"I should leave." His lips smiled but his eyes were empty.

"What if I don't want you to?"

I touched my fingertips to his forearm, the hair raspy over velvet flesh. He looked down and quickly back to me. His chuckle created goose bumps down my spine, arms and legs. I was unable to suppress the shudder from sensuous energy flooding my body.

His gaze was unfathomable. "Only a paranormal romance writer would want me to stay."

His look made me feel like the quicksand had dried around me. My outside was immobile but inside... it was as if every emotion churned in a whirlpool; pulled to the depths then thrown around in wild eddies. I'd never felt this before.

His pupils expanded briefly and, before he could turn

his head away, I thought I noticed his eyes flatten to slits. *Weird!*

The whirlpool seemed to slow as he turned away. Now it felt like I was being laid gently on the shore by an ebbing tide, emotions soothed, quicksand washed away.

I shook my head to clear it and glanced down. I saw my hand in his, fingers laced together. I hadn't felt his touch. I couldn't remember reaching out to take his hand.

He stiffened seconds before I heard the lift prowling to a stop. I didn't want to be seen talking to him in the corridor but before I could move, the doors opened and Caryn, a published author, tumbled out.

"Hey Juliette, you left ages ago. Are you lost?"

"No, just talking." I tried to sound off-hand but I knew it didn't work.

"Well, come on, your room's down next to mine."

Caryn made no mention of the stranger on my arm. I should introduce him but I didn't know his name.

We arrived at our rooms. Caryn insisted on waiting until I was safely inside. Now what do I do? She must think he's my partner and short of explaining, I had no choice but to invite him in.

I opened the door hesitantly and smiled a welcome. He lifted an eyebrow in question and I mouthed, "Come in," before turning and waving goodnight to Caryn.

The door closed. I was alone in my room with a stranger, a very delicious stranger. *What on earth am I doing?*

"Could I get you a drink, coffee, tea?" I was getting cold feet, not just feet, cold everything.

It was when he shook his head to decline, I noticed the

flush to his skin and that his topaz eyes had darkened to chocolate. *Was he aroused?*

My heart thudded to a halt. Had I invited a would-be rapist into my room? I swallowed convulsively trying not to lose the dinner I'd just consumed. It was my own fault if I ended up dead. I groaned inwardly. I was not irresponsible. I'd never before invited a man I'd just met into an intimate setting.

I wiped my sweating palms down my skirt, then stopped and balled them. I didn't want to bring attention to my legs.

His voice was normal as he broke the strained silence. "I should introduce myself. I'm Eris, and you...?"

"Juliette." My voice sounded strangled, and it was. My jaws were clenched so tightly together, words could hardly escape my lips.

His smile was like sunshine breaking through storm clouds but I couldn't afford to think like that. He could be a madman.

He swept into a low old-fashioned bow. "Juliette, lovely to meet you."

"I'm sorry. I made a mistake inviting you here. Please leave." I pointed to the doorway and took quick steps towards it.

"I mean you no harm. I just want to talk."

I stared into those shining topaz eyes and could see that he spoke honestly. I could have dropped into the depths of that gaze. The connection I felt to Eris was powerful.

"About writing?" I asked, still hearing a glitch of fear in my voice. He must have heard it too because he stepped away, leaving me a clear pathway to the door.

"Yes. How do you come up with your ideas?" He walked casually to the couch and sat with relaxed comfort—it didn't appear forced. Maybe he wasn't here for nefarious deeds. The panic slightly subsided.

"Your friend, for example, has her mind full of courtesans and risqué lords. How does she know what to write when she couldn't have lived in those times?"

I gave a hesitant, conciliatory smile. I could talk about writing. "Her books are amazing, aren't they?" Then my face pulled into a puzzled frown. "How do you know who she is?"

"I don't know her at all. I know what is in her mind."

Her mind? I scoffed and took another step closer to the door. He <u>was</u> insane. I had made a bad decision. Now I had to get him out of this room, or myself out of danger.

"I promise I won't hurt you. But I need to tell you something. Would you sit?" His voice was a soft croon. I wanted to believe him but things were just too strange.

My body was a war zone. My head was trying to make my legs run but for now, my heart was over-ruling by not sending blood to move them.

"You can tell me while I'm here." There was no way I was going to ignore my mind. I had to be near the door so I could escape if he moved any closer.

"Your friend didn't comment about me."

"I know. And I didn't know your name to introduce you. She probably thinks we're ..." My eyes widened as my brain worked. My breath became short puffs as new words rushed from my mouth. "I'll run and scream if you so much as come any closer."

"That's not what she thought." His voice was still warm honey but the tone was chilled. I waited for him to explain.

"She didn't even know I was there."

"But you were beside me. She had to know."

He moved his head in a slow shake as his chin dipped towards his chest. A defeated pose, matching his voice. "The girls in the lift... did they speak to me, notice me? Your friend?" He paused. "People don't see me."

My heart gave up for a few beats, to gather strength before stampeding. I grabbed the corner of the wall in an effort to remain standing.

"What?" It was a gasp, laden with horror and curiosity.

"You're the only one."

A huge lump blocked the scream erupting from my lungs. I dragged a heavy hand towards my mouth and wiped. Then I fisted my hand between my collarbones, pressing on the scream-blocking lump inside.

It didn't help.

"Oh, God, what does that mean?"

"You're the paranormal writer, surely you know what it means."

I stared. I wished I was any other genre writer. *Except crime.* The words popped into my mind and broke my panic-filled thoughts. If he was going to rape or kill me, surely he would have done it by now.

Pulse steadied.

The story teller came alive.

I had to understand him.

I took a step closer and extended my hand. "So, explain to me what you are and why I can see you."

"I don't know why you can see me." He sounded as confused as I felt.

"So what are you?"

His gaze wavered and he looked away. He stood and walked to the window, staring out as if seeing nothing. His voice was almost a whisper. "I'm a vampire but not a blood-sucker."

I was aghast yet compelled. Drawn by the quiet pain in his voice I walked three steps closer. "What do you drink instead?"

"Emotions. We feed on human emotion. The strongest ones are best—lust, greed, wrath, envy."

My mouth opened and closed twice before I could make a word squeak. "How?"

He shrugged. "It's mental feeding. Feeding from a person's energy."

"What? You fed from Caryn?"

"Of course, how else did I know what she writes? It was lust. Strong passionate lust." His voice had a waver to it that I thought was him feeling lust. I shuddered and took quick backward steps feeling for the edge of that wall.

"What happens when you feed? Do you erase emotions?" My voice got faster and higher as I realised the awfulness. "Oh, my god, what if Caryn can't write again? What if you've made her emotion-less?"

He laughed softly, a ripple sighing across the room. "Juliette, you're over-reacting. If we wiped out emotions, wouldn't you have heard about it? We've been feeding for centuries, it would be a well-known disease."

"How many of you are there?"

"I don't know exactly but we aren't here to hurt. We

just want to feel."

"You can't feel?"

His lip quirked up at the right corner as if unable to smile. "I am empty of emotion."

"And when you feed?"

"I am filled. I feel whole. I ride euphoria, I bask in happiness. I even enjoy despair."

"Did you feed from me?"

He shook his head. "No. I tried but it seems that you see me but I can't access your mind. It's odd. I've never come across that before."

I stared, unsure of how to react, what to say or where to go. My mind was telling me to run, fast, although a corner was intrigued by Eris and wanted to question him further. My heart, which was winning, was begging me to go to him. Hold him. He was alone and empty.

He seemed to sense my struggle. He turned to face me, stepping slowly from the window, hands extended from his sides in an open gesture.

"We're called Emotional Vampires. We're not well known."

He walked to within six feet and slowly sank to one knee. I watched warily, the war inside still waging.

"Juliette..." Eris looked up, his gaze searching my soul.

I allowed his invasion. Held his gaze voluntarily. I could see the emptiness. My fear evaporated. Anger and shock dissipated. I believed him... but I would check with Caryn tomorrow.

The need to speak was strong but the only word in my mind was his name. I didn't breathe it nor shout. It was not an invitation, dismissal or apology. It was just the word.

"Eris."

He lifted his hands and I slowly extended a hand to meet them. He didn't claim my hand, only touched my fingertips lightly. I took a step closer so my hand rested easily on his. My shoulder muscles immediately eased. There was no sparking attraction. I think I had worn out all my strong emotion. There was just tranquillity.

"As shocking as this is for you, I think that we... might... be..." Eris hesitated, as if searching for the word, or searching me to see if the word would send me fleeing.

I knew the word. I breathed it into the stillness of the room. "Soul mates?" The word hovered. Wavering between plummeting and soaring.

I walked the remaining steps until I was close enough to taste his musk and lavender scent.

"Ah, Juliette." Eris lowered his head and pressed a feather-light kiss to the back of my hand. It was like a cloud brushing against me and sparks burning into my hand all at once.

Unbelievable.

I couldn't possibly be attending my first writers' conference and meeting my soul mate, who made multiple story lines erupt in my mind.

Eris stood. His topaz gaze again plunged into my depths. He seemed to understand me even if he couldn't feed from me. He lowered his lips towards mine. In the heart beat of waiting for our lips to meet, I felt, tasted and heard his whisper. "Believe, Juliette, believe."

The End

LAST HOPE SAFARI

*M*atilda leaned against the log Jake dragged from the bush. It prickled against her back until she wriggled enough and found a comfortable spot. Not a camper, Matilda was finding Jake's outback adventure a lot less awful than she'd expected. Jake made comfortable camps and she enjoyed the home-making routines they'd developed after two weeks on the road.

Jake thought getting away from everything and tuning in with nature and each other would help them. Being with people wasn't something he enjoyed, so camping in the middle of nowhere was his perfect holiday. The opposite was true for Matilda. However, she knew they needed something to make things right.

The night was mild but she knew from her thirteen nights of experience, it would get cold. Most nights, curling up together in their double swag was not enough; she needed socks, a beanie and even a rug down the swag on the opposite side to Jake. Having Jake in bed was like having a hot water bottle that never got cold, but the non-

Jake side still froze. The fire was good until it died down, then she needed that blanket to hold in every bit of warmth.

It was delicious snuggling up with Jake beneath the diamond dusted sable sky. With the campfire crackling and embers exploding like fireworks, there was magic to the night.

'Is it the forest itself that gives off the smell or the wood we're burning?'

Jake turned from the fire, his face a mix of dark shadows and dancing colour. It was like watching a kaleidoscope. His nose appeared, then the sweep of his upper lip, the swell of his lower lip, the arch of a brow, the deep blue of his eye, the flash of white as he smiled then his teeth finally captured the light. 'I think it's both. Do you like it?'

Smiling and nodding, Matilda stretched out her arm to take the mug of billy tea Jake had just poured. That charry-tea taste was always going to remind her of these special nights.

Jake settled beside her and slipped his arm across her shoulders allowing her to burrow against him. 'Tomorrow we'll be in different country, so smell all you can now.' He sipped his tea.

Matilda felt a stir of longing for her husband. Thirteen nights of snuggling together had finally woken her interest. Nothing could explain her lack of libido. There was nothing physically wrong with her. Jake thought she was over-worked but that wasn't the reason. Always a hard worker, she'd never lost interest before. It was mental pressure - pressure to perform, to do her duty, to conceive - making her unable to be near Jake. They had been married for a few years now and everyone expected the big announcement – and it wasn't happening.

Matilda sipped her tea, her hands curled around the cup like she was grasping a life buoy. Taking her thoughts too far had killed that spark of longing. She looked into the campfire and watched the flames dance - lifting, diving, circling, weaving. It was mesmerising.

'Tonight Mt Garnet guards us. Tomorrow we're going about one hundred kilometres south-west of here.' Jake's voice was melodic, the rise and fall of his chest soothing. Matilda curled against him, listening and feeling.

The sap in a piece of burning wood sizzled, hissing sharply in the night air. Matilda held her breath while the noise vibrated through her. When she felt the breath fill her lungs to almost bursting, the wood burst apart, splattering tiny embers into the sky and across the dancing flames. Her breath expelled at the same speed.

Jake continued as if he hadn't felt her stiffen. 'They say Undara National Park has the longest lava flow in the world. There's heaps of natural caves, with areas of rainforest in the middle of the dry country.' Jake fell silent.

The bush at night is never silent, so Jake's pause allowed the sounds of the bush to dominate—the magical calls of bats and birds, the rustle of animals moving, the sizzle, crackle and pop of the fire, the soft sighing of a breeze in the leaves. Matilda let the sounds fill her with a peace she had not known existed.

'It sounds lovely.'

Matilda's murmured words seemed to break the spell that held Jake against her. He leaned down, kissed the top of her head and took her mug from her hands.

41

'I'm ready for bed. And you?' This was Jake's cue each night for Matilda. She had one rule for this safari - she was never left alone at night. Jake had faithfully maintained this promise. He kept watch while she did her nightly ablutions, prepared the swag so she could climb in sure that nothing was in there before her. The light from Jake's banked fire gave comfort until she fell asleep. Each night this routine gave her a sense of completeness, a strong bond, almost intimacy.

When they were snuggled in each other's arms, with only the stars to see them, Matilda crept her fingers along Jake's chest and jaw, before tracing the outline of his mouth. She leaned forward and pressed her lips to his. There was no pressure, no movement. Just the touch of flesh against flesh, the tiny tingling of low voltage made her aware of the connection. She curled her hand around the end of his shoulder where it pointed to the sky. As her hand clasped, her lips drew back slowly. She'd been a heart beat away from kissing him more deeply. Kissing him as a husband truly deserved.

'Thank you.' The words were a whisper between them. Matilda uttered them but she didn't know what they were for. Was she thanking him for not pressuring her? For his care? For the trip? She wasn't sure. She tucked her head down. The steady rhythm of his chest, like a calm sea, rocked her to sleep. Mt Garnet kept a solitary watch during the night.

The sharp, ear-piercing screech of a cockatoo shattered the

dream Jake had been enjoying. His body still sheltered the fragile form of his sleeping wife. He watched the dark blonde lashes flutter on her cheeks as her eyes danced to a dream. The silky tickle of her curls brushed against his face. Her legs clung to his. Her body flush against him. He wished it was because she truly desired him. He knew she desired only his warmth. A rueful smile cracked his lips allowing the cool morning air to invade his mouth.

After years of trying to conceive, Matilda had lost herself. He half understood what happened; he just couldn't find a way to be close to her. This was his last effort. If this trip didn't find the solace he needed, the spark he required for this relationship to continue... He didn't want to think beyond there. He looked down at the woman he loved. This trip had to work. The lava tubes were his last hope.

Jake lifted his eyes from Matilda and met their stationary guard, Mount Garnet. He didn't think mountains were gods, or had the power of gods, but the looming presence of this mountain seemed to call to him. He stared at the craggy rocks, the small stunted trees, the bushes hanging to precarious life. *Please, let the lava be good to us. Please, let us find ourselves again. Please help us.*

He felt Matilda stir as he finished his silent plea. He blinked, rubbed his fist against his eyes and greeted her with a smile as she woke.

'Good morning, Gorgeous.'

'Morning, Jake. Did you sleep well?'

Intimacy. This just didn't cut it for Jake.

'I slept with you. Of course I slept well.' Jake stretched his arms from the swag and pulled them upwards, fingers interlaced, stretching his shoulders. He unzipped the swag and they both crawled out into the new day.

Breakfast was routine, as was packing up the vehicle, clearing their campsite and getting on the road. Jake took the wheel and Matilda the map. They were on their way to the lava caves.

The hour drive went by quickly with casual comments about the weather, destination, road condition and passing scenery. Driving past Mt Surprise, they shared a few jokes; a glimmer of the togetherness they once shared. There were no awkward silences, nor was it particularly strained. It was like friends or family travelling. Jake just wanted more.

'I thought you said this would be rainforest?' Matilda's question was valid given the country looked as dry as everything else they'd seen. Red dirt, scattered scrub and bright blue sky.

'Hmm, I thought so too.'

They followed the signs to the lava caves. When they arrived at the Undara office, Jake gave his name and a guide appeared to take them on the tour. Matilda's eyebrow lifted in surprise.

'You organised a tour?'

Jake had organised the tour weeks before. He'd seen a picture he wanted to incorporate into a special moment for Matilda. He'd spoken with the staff and made arrangements. Matilda was in for a treat.

The caves were astounding. Larger than expected and at times it felt as if they were alone in the world. The guide walked a little ahead, allowing them to wonder, talk, and amazingly, hold hands. Jake almost stopped breathing when Matilda crept her fingers along his palm and then threaded her fingers with his. It felt wonderful to walk along these primitive tunnels, hand in hand. To have her brush close, stand so her body aligned with his, touching him, moving in synchronicity. It was almost all he'd hoped for.

They spent a couple of hours prowling through the caves, their guide pointing out one interesting fact after another, sometimes shining his torch at a phenomenal formation of geology, or the deeply dangling tree roots that penetrated fissures or rock falls. Each step brought new amazement, a new fact, a new squeeze of Matilda's fingers on his. Jake's whole body was growling for time alone with Matilda, although only his stomach growling for lunch was audible.

The guide led them through a smaller tunnel and stopped with his torch pointing at his feet. They stood before him.

'Stand here and face to your left. I'll just turn a light on the wall for you. You'll have a few moments before I need to turn the light off. We can't keep the light on this formation for long, for fear of deterioration.'

The guide left. In the dimming light, Jake could see a tiny frown marring Matilda's forehead and then the light was gone. He felt Matilda's sharp intake of breath, the sweat of her palm, the tension in her fingers. He wanted to reassure her but he didn't want her to miss the formation they were about to see.

The light came on.

Matilda gasped.

Jake stood speechless. It was more powerful seeing it in person than he'd imagined from the photograph.

He felt Matilda pull her fingers from his but she didn't

move away. Her body rocked in a manner that concerned him.

He felt for her hand, found her arm, and pulled her across the front of his body. She came willingly, pressing her back against him. He wrapped his arms around her, holding her close. He breathed in her scent.

The light went out.

He bent and whispered against his wife's ear. 'I love you, Mrs Garrett.'

Her face turned towards his, her lips brushed along his jaw. He hoped she was searching for his lips but before she found them, the torchlight of the guide came closer and she turned away.

'Isn't it amazing? A perfect heart shape etched into the rock.' The guide's voice held the same awe they'd felt.

'Is it natural?' Matilda's voice held a note of disbelief.

'Yes, perfectly natural. No one is sure how it was created. It's probably just a fluke of nature. Anyway, I have to get you out on time or I'll be in trouble.' The guide smiled to show that the trouble wouldn't be serious, but he was serious about the timing.

They came down an ever brightening tunnel towards daylight. Jake felt a certain sadness leaving the tunnel behind, but he was keen to see if the rest of his surprise was as well received.

Matilda walked into the sunlight and blinked rapidly. *No way!* There was no way she could be seeing what she was seeing. After that stunning heart, she must be imagining things. She rubbed her eyes with the heels of her hands.

Beneath a large fig tree, was a table set with a white linen cloth, gleaming glassware and silver service. A waiter stood beside a trolley of silver domed dishes. It was an oasis, or a mirage.

'This can't possibly be real,' she whispered, thinking she spoke quietly and no one would hear.

'It's real. We don't do this for all our guests, mind you.' The guide bowed, shook their hands and left them to the service of their waiter.

'Welcome,' the waiter greeted. 'If you would like to be seated, I can serve.'

And serve he did. One dish after another of her favourite foods - prawns, lobster, rack of lamb, a fresh Greek salad, roast potatoes crunchy and golden. The meal was spectacular. Then dessert; tiny scrolls of wicked chocolate, burnt fig sauce over bite-sized sticky date pudding. A cheese platter followed. Double brie, rich blue vein, quince paste, crackers, grapes and a bitey vintage rounded off the perfect feast. The white sparkling wine served was crisp and didn't smother the flavours of the food.

When they could not eat another bite, the waiter removed everything, leaving them with a blanket, some throw pillows and three hours of siesta.

'This is heaven.' Matilda spread the blanket beneath the shady fig, dumped a pile of pillows and lay back in dreamy delight. She patted the space beside her, beckoning Jake.

He lay staring into the vastness of the blue sky, fig leaves causing dapples of sunlight to scurry across his features. Matilda felt her heart swell. This was the man she loved.

This man who gave her space, everything she asked for, all the love and protection he could give. This man was hers. But before she could claim him, she had a bridge to build. She only hoped she hadn't left it too long.

She leaned up on her elbow and stared at her husband, tracing his face with her gaze while she spoke.

'Jake Garrett, did you organise all of this?'

He made a sound like a hum, an affirmative response.

'Am I worth it?' Matilda heard the tentativeness in her voice. She'd surprised herself with the words. She meant to say she loved him. Not ask him if she was worth it. What if he said no? What if he hated her? What if she'd pushed him too far already?

Deep down, she knew she hadn't. She knew it was close but she still had time, maybe only a short time, like the two days left of their holiday.

Jake sat up and drew her to him. He took her face gently between his palms, as if examining the finest glass.

'Yes. You're worth everything to me.' His voice was sure, steady and solid, reflecting what she saw in his eyes, and in the set of his jaw.

She gulped.

He released her.

She didn't want him to let her go. She reached out, one hand against his shoulder, the other cradled his cheek and jaw. She leaned forwards so her lips almost brushed against his. She could feel the delicate puff of his breath. It made her lips ache.

'The heart on the rock wall was beautiful, Jake. It's the most beautiful thing I've ever seen. How did you get them to do it?'

'It really is natural. I saw a picture. I wanted you to see it. They don't usually show people but I made a good case, and they allowed us to see.'

'You made a case?'

Jake looked a little sheepish. 'I lied. I told them I wanted to propose. They came up with the lunch, the relaxing afternoon.'

Matilda laughed. Only Jake would create such a romantic lie. Jake, her crazy, wonderful, thoughtful, caring, loving husband.

'I love you, Jake Garrett. And yes, I will marry you, a hundred times over.' Matilda leaned forward and initiated their kiss. She didn't kiss like she had over the last months. She kissed like when they dated, with the reckless abandon of a teenager. She kissed her husband with all the passion she'd lost.

And he returned her kiss, equally.

In the dappled sunlight, under the watchful gaze of a large fig tree, lying on the most fertile soils of Australia, Mr and Mrs Garrett created their own history. In nine months time they'll understand the fertility of the lava tubes and the protection of Mount Garnet.

The End

DIAMOND SHIELD

This story was first published in the Little Gems Diamond Short Story Anthology 2012, by Romance Writers of Australia.

*I*t's work. It's work. It's work. The mantra spins through my mind during the five minute intervals that each of the four men sit before me. Speed dating. Good grief! The bell can't ring quickly enough. Each man is a boring replica of the one before. I miss nothing by skipping the dating game.

The fifth man arrives. I smile the first genuine smile of the night. Mr Sex-on-Legs saunters to my table. His dark buzz cut, angular face, lush lips and graceful movement on a hugely athletic body stirs every nerve ending. The hairs on the back of my neck stand up and quick-march down my spine.

Delicious.

One glance at my name tag and he gives a short sharp bark of denial. "Dia Monde? You can't be serious. Are you related to Saph Ire?" An eyebrow lifts saucily as his jade gaze drills me. His name tag reads 'Mitch' but is that any more real than mine?

Two gems. He mentioned two gems. Please no. He can't be my contact. Contacts should be sleazy men, not sex-on-legs.

"I don't know a Saph Ire. But I do know an Emma Rald." My mention of the third gem should lead him to asking about my profession. *Please don't ask. Please don't ask. Please don't ask.*

He laughs and this time it's a husky sound that ripples through my body and I forget all about this being work. "Is she related to O Pal and Rube Bee?"

More gems, not the contact. Relief floods me but at the same time, I'm miffed that this guy, who is too good looking to be doing the dating game, can sit and laugh at me. "Are we going to do this all night?" I sound like a shrew.

"I was hoping we'd have much better things to do tonight than trade insults."

The suggestive tone has my heart galloping and my mind moving towards wicked. He doesn't wait for an answer, just winks as my face heats, and continues the conversation. "So, let me guess, you're seriously into lapidary?"

"No, I work in a shoe store." I give the answer I'm supposed to give my contact because I can't think of anything else. The barest hint of his tongue poked between his teeth as he waited for my answer and my mind turned to mush.

He leans across the small table, one finger pressing against his lips and I'm trapped in the spell he weaves. Breath caught. Heart fluttering. Palms sweating.

"You don't dabble in gems on the side?" he asks.

"No."

Five times his finger touches his lip and an armed holdup right here, right now could not draw my eyes away. Hands are my 'thing' and his fit every requirement. Strong. Nicely shaped fingers. Clean nails, not bitten not overly manicured. A working hand that's cared for. His solid finger presses against his full, decidedly kissable lips. I lean closer as if pulled by his aura.

We banter about shoes, jewellery, fitness, dating. My skin prickles throughout. I sense an undercurrent I'm missing but I shrug off my apprehension. It's probably because I'm enjoying myself, and this is supposed to be work.

After failing to agree on the best first date, we chuckle at each other and then lapse into silence. A full silence that magnifies his every breath, the blink of his eyes and the softening of his lips.

His husky voice makes me jump. "Diamonds are much too cold and impersonal for you. You're a gem with fire, passion. A red opal. Slashes of red fire in darkness."

His assessment makes my blood chill. He's shattered the silence and my enjoyment.

"And you know this within minutes of meeting me?" I'm back to being a nasty shrew but he doesn't seem to notice. The bell rings.

Leaning across the table he crowds my personal space. I long to move closer and that's a foreign feeling. His predatory green eyes lure me. I'm holding my breath as he speaks.

"I know so much more than you can imagine."

He leans back and walks from my table. Cool air hits me but it has nothing to do with the shiver running through me. He left. He left and I don't understand. How can he know me?

I sit through another man, two, while I'm trying to understand. My mind's not on the job. Before I'm aware of the contact, he's made the three gemstone mentions and asked me about my work. My cop mode switches on. Understanding 'Mitch' is on hold. I make the correct responses and sit through inane chatter with the sleaze-bag until the bell rings. He extends his hand and I remember to shake it without flinching. The microchip, along with a fist full of sweat, are in my palm. He leaves. I wish I could run but only half the job's done. Mr Sex-on-Legs has got under my guard and I don't like it.

Grabbing my glass I gulp the rest of the water. Shame it's nothing stronger. I have to endure another couple of dates.

My boss, Joe, is my final date.

"How did you go?"

"I have what we need." Meaning I have the microchip containing secret information.

"Excellent. And your dates?" He grins as if it's a private joke. But then it probably is. If the women here were as bad as the men, he's had as bad a night as I.

"The dates. Goodness. I have a swag of cards to shred."

"All of them?" He lifts an eyebrow as he slides his card to me. I take it, slipping it into my handbag with all the others. How many women will ring his bogus number?

I grin mischievously at him. "This card I'll keep. Maybe frame it in the office." He's been antsy about this job. It's a favour for his mate, approved through Headquarters, and what's more, his wife is worried about him doing the speed dating game, which was considered the safest way to make contact—whoever's stupid idea that was.

When the bell rings on the final interview, Joe leans across the table. "See you soon."

We're meeting back at the office and I go right there. I don't want to mix with the dates for drinks afterwards. Well, I do. I want to mix with Mr Sex-on-Legs but I can't. I'm a cop, not a shoe shop girl. And he's wrong about his red opal. I am a cold impersonal diamond. I'd rather he never know.

I beat Joe back to work. While I'm waiting I pull the business cards from my bag and dump them on the desk. I leave the microchip where it is. It's safer in my bag and won't get shredded by mistake. Joe'll put it in the evidence locker when he gets here. I make a pile of the cards before picking them up and shuffling them on my way to the shredder.

One of them is written on. I stop and fan the cards out, pulling the one with writing on the back. I flip them over. A second with writing. I place the cards on the corner of the desk while I dump the rest in the rubbish bin. I look back at the cards.

The first is written in Joe's scrawl. 'You're a gem. Thanks!'

The second is not Joe's scrawl. 'I heard you were a gem. I'm not disappointed.'

Who the hell was that? Someone else was undercover? Someone else in that line up of men knew what was happening tonight? Joe kept me in the dark?

I hear Joe before I see him and stalk to the doorway. "You lied to me, Joe. You had someone else in there."

"Gees, keep you shirt on, Kendra."

Joe's not going to pacify me this time. "Since when do we go in only knowing half the facts?"

"Since I asked him to keep quiet." This deep voice is new but somewhat familiar. I look beyond Joe and in the gloom of the stairwell stands the sexy lapidarist.

"Oh, hell! I might have guessed you were involved."

Joe shoots me a warning look, or a look of concern, I can't read it because ninety nine point nine per cent of my attention is on the man behind him.

"Spill, or no microchip." I stand my ground, barring the doorway, legs shoulder-width apart, hands on my hips and my well-schooled obstinate expression on my face. My brothers taught me this cold hard stare.

"Coffee first." The sexy stranger walks past Joe and skirts around my immobile body, unaffected by my stare. "Those women were the pits, except one sexy little gem."

Joe laughs but I quell that with a glance.

I spin around and stalk after the object of my frustration. "Don't think sweet talking is going to fix things."

My heart beat's much too rapid. His hips sway with his loping motion. The tight globes of his butt become the centre of my focus. The globes move and flex in a rhythmic dance that has me spellbound. There's no moisture in my mouth. Every drop has headed south.

"No, but sweet coffee might help."

I drag my eyes from his butt but he's still facing the coffeepot. I'm sure he's been ogled by far more women than I can guess at, but I don't want to get caught.

He pours two coffees and dumps three sugars into one, two in the other. I turn around but Joe's nowhere to be seen. "Chicken," I mutter under my breath.

"Here." He passes me the two sugared coffee. He must read my unasked question. "Joe told me how you take it."

"What hasn't Joe told you?" I move to my desk and perch on the corner. I need distance from this man.

"Yeah, sorry. It is a bit one-sided." He sticks his hand out towards me in a friendly gesture. "I'm Major Mitchell Doyle, Australian Army, a friend of Joe's from way back."

My stomach rapidly sinks to my knees. Mitch Doyle, the man I dubbed Mr Dynamite for his ability to blow off women.

"Joe's mentioned you."

"Oh yeah? What did he say?" Mitch grew in stature, if that's possible. His shoulders draw back as he cocks his head to one side.

"Nothing flattering, so don't get excited." I make my voice a low drawl, hoping it will mask the tense, keyed up energy hovering inside me.

I lied. Joe always speaks well of Mitch. My interpretation made him out to be Mr Dynamite. And that was built on three years of Joe trying to set me up with this guy. I guess, tonight, he succeeded.

"Kendra, you haven't seen me excited...yet." The lure of

his voice is hypnotic and with the promise lying beneath those words, I almost melt off my desk. But I have six brothers—I know every trick men use to get what they want and I'm not falling for this.

May as well fight fire with fire. "Mitch, with your lifestyle, I doubt I could get you excited."

He prowls closer and I'm pinned to the desk by his stare. Another tactic.

"Nothing excites me more than a fiery red opal encased in diamond." He leans towards me, his face millimetres from mine. His eyes refuse to allow mine to skitter away. I'm trapped and I like it. Coffee warmed breath drifts across my lips. They part and my tongue slips along them trying to find moisture. My lips tingle with the warmth of his breath. I draw in a deep breath, as if I'm readying to dive underwater. I'm filled with the heady scents of coffee, rich spice and strong male. He's good enough to eat.

A deep guttural groan snaps my head away from his, and I lean back towards my bag. "Don't you need the microchip?"

I hope like heck it was his groan I heard and not mine.

I called Joe a chicken before but it's me now needing the title. Mitchell Doyle sets every button in my body alight. It's like he has the override key to my senses and there isn't a thing I can do to control them.

"I'm needing you, Kendra." He pauses as if letting me digest this statement. "The microchip was a convenient excuse."

His hold on me snaps.

"I'm not part of the deal." Jumping off the table I snatch my bag, holding it in front of me like a shield. I place the microchip on the table and take one last look at him before I flee.

I'm two flights down the stairs before he catches me. He grabs my arm like my brothers do, hauling me to a halt.

"The job was real. I had to get the chip. It contains sensitive national security information. And the contact requested the speed dating set up." He holds my gaze and his honesty is difficult to ignore.

"Why did you need me?"

His hold on my arm isn't hurting, but it holds all my attention. His calloused hand rubs my skin, yet I'm not sure he's moving. Heat seeps into me from his body. And those damn eyes hold me captive. Big cat eyes that hold so much raw emotion I almost fall into their depths.

"I've been waiting to meet you for three years. Joe's tried to organise it so many times I've forgotten. You're the most elusive woman I've ever known."

"So?" I'm elusive, so what? He's dynamite.

"I need a strong, independent woman. I'm sick of meeting insipid ones who fawn over me. I'm sick of the dating scene."

I must have betrayed my disbelief because he gives a short sharp burst of laughter.

"You can't possibly have enjoyed the dating scene tonight?" he says.

Aside from his banter, nothing about tonight was enjoyable. Giving the tiniest conciliatory smile I admit, "I hated it."

"See, that's why we need to get to know each other. We both hate games. You're strong enough to handle a bunch of men and earn their respect. That can't be easy. Joe does nothing but sing your praises. Even his wife thinks we'd be suitable."

I snort, breaking into his argument. "She only wants me off the market. All the wives do."

He grins and my traitorous stomach flips.

"Oh, so you know the wife-vibe." He speaks as if we share an intimate secret.

"How can I not? It's like the most powerful vibe on earth..." I hesitate before muttering under my breath, "...the second most."

Mitch frowns. "And the most...?"

My lips twitch before I spin on the stairs, determined to lose his hold and head home, away from the most powerful vibe.

"No escaping." The low, deep, throaty murmur stops me dead. Now that's the most powerful vibration I've heard.

And I succumb. To the vibration, the raw emotion and the attraction.

Mitch Doyle walks down the stairs until we're eye-to-eye. "What do you say, friends?"

My lips curl into a smile. "I'm betting you don't have female friends."

He touches his index finger to my chin, just below my bottom lip. How I wish he'd move it higher but he doesn't. He stares at my mouth. "You're right. But who's to say you can't be the first."

I walk a tiny step closer so our shoes touch and there's barely a breath between us. "I could be the first."

Neither of us moves. Our gazes lock.

Finally he glances down to my mouth. My lips throb

from the attention. His finger slides slowly beneath my lip. My hand trails across his chest.

"What exactly do female friends do?" His voice is a whisper.

"They never kiss."

His eyes flick back to mine. The green has darkened to almost black.

"Hell. I'll make a lousy friend. It's not worth it."

My laugh bursts from me as his free arm snares me around the waist and he hauls me against him. Body against body, from the toes up. I feel each part connect. And then his lips touch mine. At first it's slow and soft, like sinking into a feather pillow. But that lasts seconds. Our kiss ignites like dynamite. Explosions rip through my body. I can't get enough of his taste. Sweet coffee with a hint of mint. I lean into him, urging him on. His lips catch, caress and demand. I'm not content to let him control this. I slip my tongue against his lips, firing the kiss to the next level. It's all I can do to suck in the air I need to stay alive.

The heat simmers down, and we're left touching tiny kisses against each other's lips. He pulls back by the barest margin and I miss the contact.

"Kendra, I hate to say I'm right but that hard diamond shield you wear just melted with that kiss." He smirks as if he's had the last word.

"Don't you know, diamond's the toughest thing on earth. I lowered my shield. One false move and it'll be back." I hold his gaze, not letting him get the better of me.

But he won't give me the last word.

"I never make a false move." His lips punctuate the claim and I'm happy to let time be the judge.

The End

FAREWELL SAPPHIRE

*S*apphire is a tiny town in Queensland, home to
550 people, give or take the tourists, and me.
Our closest town is Emerald, and our greatest claim to
fame is the gem fields surrounding the area. Some
imaginative soul named the towns around here—Emerald,
Sapphire, Rubyvale. I often wonder if he found a Sapphire
here and that's why he called it so, or if he just wished
he had.

I've lived here all my life and have planned my escape
for almost as long. As far as small towns go there's nothing
wrong with Sapphire. I want to live in a larger town, or even
a city. I dream of Brisbane, or Sydney or Melbourne. In my
youth, I had scrapbooks filled with magazine and
newspaper photographs of these Australian cities. Now I've
moved on. New York, Paris, Rome, London or Perth capture
my attention now.

Imagine living in Perth…. Still in Australia, but miles
from other capitals. It'd be like a country on its own. A river
through the city that never dries up. The ocean at your

western shore. And the whole continent between my new abode and Sapphire.

Mum and Dad run the Sapphire Caravan Park and we've worked in it since time began. There's five of us. I'm the eldest. Then my sister, Emmie, two brothers, who got normal names, Harry and Jack, and our baby sister, Ruby. I tried to gloss over the girls names but you can't gloss over Ruby. Emmie is Emerald but we never call her that. I bet you can't guess my name... yep... no prizes, Sapphire. Sapphire in Sapphire. What were they thinking? I get called Sappy when I'm teased, but Saph mostly.

See why I hate being here?

If I was Sapphire in Sydney, it would be a beautiful name, especially teamed with my bright blue eyes. But Sapphire in Sapphire with sapphire eyes—seriously!

Anyway, tomorrow I'm eighteen. And eighteen is the age I promised I'd leave town. I amended it from sixteen when Emmie sobbed and told my parents the day before my birthday. Now everyone in town knows I'm leaving. No secrets here. Emmie's still sobbing but as I've tried to tell her, Emerald in Sapphire isn't half so bad.

The most difficult part about leaving is physically getting away from town. The bus stops in Emerald, which is fifty five kilometres away, but there's no bus in Sapphire. So, do I hitch or walk? I can't walk. Not only is that too far but my birthday's February so I'd never be able to carry enough water to survive the summer sun baking me.

There are a heap of grey nomads going through town. And the Caravan Park's the perfect place to pick them up. I've sussed out a few of them and the general vibe is that they won't take me. They all have rebellious kids and grandkids, so they think they're doing the right thing. My folks won't talk to them. They say it's my plan I have to carry it through. Fat lot of good they are. All I need them to say is that it's okay. But no. They don't really want me to leave. They'll lose their best cleaner.

I have one hope. One hope buried deep in my chest and I'm not sure I can even write it down. If I write it, my dream will vanish. So I'll keep it secret. But don't be shocked if tomorrow there's a surprise for me... a huge surprise.

I walk into breakfast and everyone sings Happy Birthday. Mum puts a huge plate of scrambled eggs in front of me and Dad drops two bits of bacon on top. Emmie butters toast and sits it alongside. Birthdays are a big deal in my family.

"Thanks, everyone." I gave Mum and Dad a big hug each. I grin at Emmie but she's sulking still, even if she did make me toast.

Breakfast is the precursor to an extended birthday. Because we're so busy in the mornings, checking people out and cleaning, the gift giving and cake waits until after lunch. So breakfast is the sampler as we all wait for the exciting part.

Once breakfast is done, I'm off to clean rooms and the boys clean camp sites. Emmie cleans rooms too but we don't work together. We work from different directions and when we meet, we're done. The morning travels along fairly well but butterflies have taken residence in my stomach. You kind of know why, but I can't tell you anymore. I sneak glances out the front of the Caravan Park whenever I can, but nothing changes. Each time I look my heart's in my throat taking out all the air. Then when nothing's there, it drops back to my rib cage and air rushes in. Lucky I'm young or I'd think I was having a heart attack.

When I meet Emmie at the last room, we clean it together. When it's sparkling and I close the door behind us, I'm laughing a maniacal chuckle.

"Oh my God, Emmie. That's my last room. Ever. Ever and ever. Amen." I grab her around the waist and twirl her but she's not excited like me, she's sobbing.

"I don't want you to go, Saph. I don't want you to leave me here."

I tilt her chin up. "When you're eighteen Emmie, I'll come and get you and take you to live with me."

"But that's two years away." She says it like it's a life sentence.

I chuck my curled finger beneath her chin. "It's only as long as I've waited since you ratted me out last time."

Emmie hangs her head and her sobs reduce to sniffles. "I'm not sorry." She says, defiant even when distressed.

We pack away the gear and clean up ready for lunch. "He won't come, you know."

I whirl on Emmie, eyes blazing, fists clenched tight so my nails dig into my palms. I can't say a word. I stalk into the house for lunch.

How dare she?

How. Dare. She.

I suck in big deep breaths trying to tamp down my fury. I'm almost gulping, like a great big carp chucked up on the riverbank.

I don't wait for Emmie to shower first. I hog the

bathroom. I scrub and wash, for the last time in this horrid bathroom. I wrap myself in the tiny scratchy towel and go to our bedroom to dress. My stuff's packed ready to go. I've left a yellow sundress out so I'm happy and bright and cheery as I leave. I slip it on.

I almost bought the sapphire coloured sundress. I thought Sapphire, leaving Sapphire, wearing sapphire would have been more memorable, but yellow looks better on me with my tanned skin. And I can't turn up in a bigger town looking silly. I've got to turn up the best I can.

Lunch is a feast. Mum's done a heap of different salads and a chook. It's my favourite summer meal. After gorging on salads, a huge chocolate mud cake appears. A sparkler shoots dazzling light while everyone sings again. The cake is delicious. Mum's a great cook. We all have seconds.

And then the gifts. Emmie, Harry, Jack and Ruby have all chipped in and bought me something. A small gaudily-wrapped box is laid into my hands with much ceremony. I slip off the ribbon and tear open the paper. A jeweller's box. When I open it, a large light blue sapphire gleams in a platinum setting. The pendant I'd admired in the shop a few months back. The pendant with the most stunning sapphire I've ever seen. It cost them a fortune. I'm speechless. Looking from one expectant face to the next, I realise they're waiting for my reaction and until now I've been too stunned to have one.

I burst into tears. Emmie does too. Ruby grabs my arm. Harry and Jack roll their eyes.

"I love it. Thank you. I'll wear it all the time." I hug each of them in turn, squeezing Emmie extra because I know she organised this.

Dad puts the pendant on for me and everyone stares at it. "It matches your eyes." Emmie's words are breathed out in awe.

"Perfectly." Mum says in the same sort of breath.

When I look in the mirror though, all I see are bloodshot eyes from crying. I'll have to check it out later. For now I'll believe them because it's the most beautiful sapphire in the world.

Mum and Dad hand me a card. "We thought this would be the most useful thing." Dad's voice is serious but a bit choked up.

Inside the card is a cheque. A cheque for more money than I've ever seen.

"No. No." I shake my head. "You can't give me this much." It's two thousand dollars.

Mum's hand closes on my upper arm. "Love, it won't go far when you're on your own."

Dad smiles. "And it's not anywhere near how much work you've done here."

"Thank you. This is the best birthday ever." I mean it. I give them all a hug again. I love my family. They're all so special. But as much as I love them, I can't stay here.

The bell in the office rings. No one jumps to get it but everyone glances at everyone else, like someone's supposed to get it.

I stand up. "I'll get it." I rub my hands over my eyes, hoping they don't look all bleary, and walk out to the office to book in whoever is early.

Opening the office door, I stop still. Dead still. The door's about a quarter way open. My body's stopped beside it unable to fit through, but I can't shut it either because my feet are in the way. But I'd never shut it.

My ride's here.

"Darren." The word comes out like a whisper. Then everything inside me gathers together tightly before springing forwards in a whirl of body parts. My voice finds itself and I call out his name, loudly, with every bit of happiness and hope I've held onto for two years. "Darren."

The counter vanishes and I'm in his arms, whirling around the front of the office so fast that brochures fly into the air.

"Happy Birthday, Saph."

"Oh my God. Darren, you came." Not that I doubted him, not ever. Not once. Never. Not a tiny bit. "You're here."

"I'm late. Did I miss the cake?" He's laughing at me. He's laughing with me. He hasn't taken his hands off my waist yet, even though he's stopped twirling me, and it's probably just as well as I don't know if my knees will hold me upright.

"We saved you a piece," Mum says from behind me. When I look around they're all there. Like they were expecting him. Like they had more faith in him arriving than I did.

"Did you plan this?" I ask, staring at Mum.

"Honey, you planned this two years ago. It's not my doing. But if you don't want to go—"

"No. I'm going." I don't want her to have the tiniest shred of a doubt. "But I'll come back to visit. And this will always be home." I fly to Mum and hug her. Then I hug

Dad, and Emmie, and Harry, and Jack, and Ruby. "I'm ready to go."

Dad laughs. "Saph, Darren needs a break. You don't know how long he's been driving."

I turn around to Darren ready to apologise. "No, Mr Jenson. I stayed at Mum and Dad's last night, so I'm ready to rock and roll."

"I'm ready too." I can't keep my teeth inside my lips. I have this Cheshire cat grin that won't leave.

"I'll pack you some food," Mum says as I race to the bedroom for my backpack.

When I fly back to Darren after a brief farewell to my room of eighteen years and a stop to grab my gifts from the lounge room, we wait for Mum to appear with food. Mum never lets you drive anywhere without a water bottle of iced water and a foam esky of food.

After a whirl of hugs, kisses, farewells and tears, Darren and I are on the road. I wind down the window and hang out to wave goodbye to my family. I show two fingers to Emmie, not as a bird, but to remind her of my promise. I'll keep it just as Darren kept his. When we get to the town limits, I wave farewell to the sign, and scream, "See you, Sapphire."

And then, exhausted, I fall into my seat. It's like all the air has sucked from me. Like I was only alive in Sapphire and I'm dying as I leave but I know that's not true because I've left Sapphire before for holidays and survived.

"It's just adrenalin, Saph. You'll be right in a bit."

"I can't believe you came, Darren. I dreamed and I hoped but you never said and so I didn't say anything."

His hand slides over mine and squeezes lightly. "Saph,

we've been dreaming of this for thirteen years. And the last two years have been hell without you. I can't wait to show you Brisbane. I can't wait to travel south."

"Why didn't you say something about coming?"

"I promised your folks I wouldn't push you into going."

I close my eyes. "They never believed I wanted to leave. Even when I said it a hundred and fifty million times, they always thought you were the bad influence because you were older."

Darren laughs. "Little did they know..."

I know it's illegal, I know I shouldn't do it, but I do it anyway. I take off my seat belt and wriggle over to Darren. My hand slips on his shoulder and I kiss his cheek. I press lots of little kisses to his cheek. The little kisses move closer and closer to the side of his mouth. I haven't kissed him in so long.

There's a bounce or two as Darren pulls the car off the road and stops it. Then my lips catch his. It's as if I kissed him yesterday, but sweeter than if I'd never kissed him before. His mouth moves beneath mine, like a ballet. We sip tiny tastes of each other until we need to feast. Then the kiss becomes wild and wickedly wonderful. I'm glad he's pulled over so I can taste him without worrying about the police. He tastes of Darren and nothing has ever tasted this good, not even Mum's chocolate cake.

When our kiss slows, he sets me back into my seat. "Saph, if you do any more of that, we'll never get out of the gem fields."

Laughing, I do my seatbelt up. Darren does his and starts the car. We move off. "How far will we get to tonight?"

"At least Gladstone, maybe even Bundaberg."

"And how long to Brisbane?"

"Another day."

Another day to city. Another day to reach our city starting point.

"In two years I have to go back and get Emmie."

Darren nods. "But we have two years to find our city, Saph. Two years to establish ourselves, or to travel, or to move about."

As his ute eats the kilometres, I call a toast out the open window. "To the future!"

The End

MOONSTONE MADNESS

"*The* winner of the raffle is...Katrina Jaclynn."

My breath expels in a huge gust that ruffles Audrey's hair as I grab her. "I won, I won." My screaming is breathy because I'm gasping and jumping up and down like a six year old. "I won a horse. I own a horse. I won a horse. Can you believe?"

That's me, twenty years older than I'm acting, but I can't help myself. It's been a lifelong dream to own a horse and now I've won one in a raffle. I never win raffles. My life is changing.

Audrey patiently waits while my excitement works its way through my system. She guides me to the Chairman or the President or whoever he is who needs to make a presentation. She listens, takes hold of the paperwork, ushers me where I have to go. My ears are ringing with the sound of my name. My heart's thudding as if I've been in a race. My skin's prickling with sweat from the heat and also the excitement. I don't think my lungs have drawn a deep breath since I heard the announcement.

It's a haze until I'm led into the horse stall area and come face to face with the most beautiful grey mare and a young, ruggedly handsome, laid-back country horseman who bred, owned, donated and trains her.

But first, the horse. She's grey, tall, beautiful. Not just grey but a silvery colour with threads of black and white streaking across her body, like marble. Her nostrils flare and she snorts as we move closer. Her ears dart forwards and back, eyes flicking all around as if she's trying to work out what's happening. It's probably my excitement she can feel. I can't stop it bubbling. I hold my hand towards her and she sniffs me, whiskers brushing across my flesh, then she snorts hot air. In a flash, she lunges, I squeal and jump backwards, right as Mr Horseman steps between me and her. He catches me, arms wrap around my waist to steady me.

Oh, dear lord, he smells of horse, hay, and soap. I draw another deep breath as my body presses against his. Not just soap, that crisp tang of male, a dash of citrus, and maybe something like cedar or sandalwood. He's lean, strong and so much male.

In a few seconds, Audrey has me out of the way and catches my arm in a death squeeze. The tension tells me, I'm making an idiot of myself. Audrey's good at the subtle gestures to keep me in line, although the nail marks on the underside of my arm might tell you this one isn't so subtle a gesture.

When Mr Horseman has my stunning grey mare settled again, he turns toward us. A blue-blue gaze, the colour of the sky on a perfect summer's day, spears me. I can't move. My breath snags in my lungs. My feet plant in the red dust.

His face is angular, sharp, thin, tanned. Not stunningly

attractive, but not unattractive. And then the eyes. And lips. Oh, his lips are like the plumpest pillows, the colour of ripe blood plums. Too decadent for the angular face. Too decadent for a man.

Dark curly hair protrudes from the back of his cap, long and untamed. It doesn't fit with the angular features, but goes perfectly with those sinful lips. Bedroom eyes, sinful lips, wild hair. Oh, my. Every drop of moisture, not whipped away by the heat of the day, has migrated south.

"You must be Katrina and Jacqueline," he says, while my mind is still stalled.

Audrey laughs. "No, I'm Audrey, her friend. She's Katrina, last name Jaclynn." She holds out her hand as she introduces herself and he shakes her hand softly. "Although, she's kind of wild and crazy, so it's like she's two people sometimes." Audrey grins at him while her elbow stabs into my ribs.

I hold my hand out. "Sorry. I've always wanted to own a horse." His hand closes around mine and it's rough and soft, strong and gentle. My gaze snags his and I start to babble. "Since I was a kid I've wanted a horse. And now I've won one, and she was yours. I can't believe it. Is this her? I've won—"

Audrey stands on my toes and I shut my mouth but still his hand holds mine. Then he looks down at our joining and does a little shake before we break free.

"I'm Josh. And this is Moonstone Madness." He doesn't say much but his voice licks through me turning my blood to something thick and warm that chugs through my system.

"She's racing today?" Audrey asks when she sees I'm incapable of a coherent thought. Lucky I've known here since I was three. Audrey's pulled me out of more jams than I can remember.

He nods. "In the second last."

"Should we bet on her?" Audrey asks again while I stand staring between the man and the horse.

"She should do well but anything can happen. She seems relaxed now, but she could get het up and ruin her chances."

Audrey smiles and grabs hold of my elbow. "I'll keep Kat away. She's a walking fount of excitement."

Josh laughs as Audrey tugs me away, then he calls out. "I'll be watching the race near the winning post if you want to meet me there."

Audrey pulls me away from the horse stalls to the canteen where she grabs cold water and sandwiches. She hauls me to a table and sits me down. "Gees, Kat. Sometimes you make me totally embarrassed to be your friend. What just happened there? Man or horse?"

I gulp half the bottle of water in one go. "Both." I put the lid on slowly and sit the bottle on the table while I grasp inside my mind for coherent thoughts.

I reach out for Audrey's hand. "I'm sorry I embarrassed you. I'm sorry I always embarrass you but I'm very glad you're with me and rein me in. Always. Sorry."

Audrey smiles and clutches my hand. "Lucky I know you well." She doesn't have to tell me that Josh doesn't know me at all and my first impression is one of complete stupidity and nonsense.

After we've eaten, Audrey wanders off to the ladies and then to chat to some of her friends. I've assured her I'll be fine here but I have another plan.

I weave my way through people, past the bookmakers and punters, around the mounting yard and back to the horse stalls. I walk along until I find Josh and Moonstone Madness. I stand quietly, away from them both, waiting until I can catch Josh's eye. Before too long, the horse snickers and Josh turns.

"Hey."

"Hey, yourself," I reply before taking a step closer. "I wanted to apologise. For earlier." I hate making apologies. I bite my lips and shift my head to the side before adding, "I can be a right fool sometimes. Sorry if I upset you or the horse."

Josh smiles when I start my apology and by the time I've finished, he's grinning. "Katrina, I work with thoroughbreds every day of my life. I'm used to it."

I frown, not quite sure if he's accepted my apology with a compliment or an insult.

"Come over here. You can meet your horse. I think you've both got a lot in common."

And I still don't know what he means but I walk close to him and the horse. "Do you call her something besides Moonstone Madness? It's kind of a mouthful."

"M. That's what I call her. Moonstone Madness is her racing name and we never use them in the stables." He walks beside her, stroking her neck with his palm and scratching her ear with his fingers. "You can give her a pat. She does a lot of crazy things, but she doesn't bite."

I smile and can't resist temptation. "Sometimes I bite."

Josh laughs and the sound goes right through me. It's deep, rumbly and completely sexy. "Well, try to refrain from biting M. I don't want her learning bad habits."

I smile and touch M's cheek. Warm hair tickles my fingers, honed muscles press against my hand. I stroke softly and she leans into my touch, so I rub a bit harder. "Does she like that?" I whisper.

"She's a glutton for attention, however it comes."

"I can totally understand, M." I stroke her, feeling more grounded than ever before. She's leaning her face on my hand, her warm body heating my front. Josh's body beside mine, warming my side. I've only met them both but I could curl up here and enjoy their presence for a long time.

"Is her name because of her colour and nature?"

Josh makes a huff. "No. She's not mad. She's rather quiet really. Although her colour is like a moonstone, I agree." He shifts his feet so he's leaning closer to me. "Her sire is Fastnet Rock and her dam is Fuming. It kind of went together. She's dappled, so a grey-white rock or gemstone, and madness is like fuming."

"Hey, that's clever."

"Thank you." We smile at each other, gazes lock.

I turn away first. "Did you name her?"

"Yes, and I don't mean to be rude but I have to get her ready soon."

I step away from him and M, after giving her one last pat and a silent wish for luck. "Sorry to keep you."

He touches my hand lightly. "You have to stop apologising, Kat. I told you I'm used to these leggy beauties and you don't seem much different." His gaze shifts along my body as if he's flirting with me. I take a step back.

"Thank you, I think."

His deep sexy laugh has my toes curling. "It was meant as a compliment, every time."

I smile then, really smile. He is flirting. "Good luck. I'll see you for the race. At the winning post, right?"

He nods. "See you there."

It takes forever until her race. Standing at the mounting yard when the horses come in before the race, I'm impatient to see them, excited to have a runner, and scared something might go wrong. When she's not the first horse in the yard, I begin to fret. And then I see them, finally, walking around outside the yard in giant circles.

It's a bit hard not to see them. Josh is in a yellow shirt that draws your attention. I mean the colour. But then the fit. His shoulders are wide, stretching the shirt across the top so bunches of fabric tuck messily into low slung jeans on slim hips. *Wow! How did I not notice?* His jeans are well-worn, hanging off his hips as if they're a coat hanger made for them. And his legs run for miles under those jeans.

"Hey, your horse." Audrey slides in beside me. "Are you nervous?"

I nod. "And excited, and speechless. Almost."

Audrey laughs. "You're never speechless."

The jockeys come out. One in yellow is heading towards M. I'll surely be able to see her now. Bright yellow with a white diagonal cross. Nice colours. Within moments, the horses are being led out onto the track and let go. Audrey grabs my arm and heads to the fence opposite the finish line.

"We have to get a good position." And we do. Right on the fence, just past the post.

The hairs on the back of my neck begin to prickle. I turn slowly and Josh is right behind me. Smiling, I shuffle along to make room but a large hand on my shoulder stills me.

"It's okay. You guys stay at the fence and I'll look over your shoulder."

I'd like him to be next to me, but since he's close behind with his hand on my bare shoulder, I'm not going to complain but savour the moment.

It seems to take forever for the horses to get around to the start, and then load in the barriers. At each passing moment, the tension in me increases. By the time the race caller tells us, 'the light's flashing and they're ready to jump', I'm ready to ping through the air like an over-stretched elastic band.

When they jump, Josh's hand squeezes my shoulder tight and it remains. Even as I'm stretching over the fence to see the horses run up the straight, his hand is there, squeezing and releasing, clenching tightly to me. His body is wrapped over mine, stretched out so he can see over my shoulder. It stops me leaping but doesn't stop me screaming. I'm hoarse as I scream for M.

And she's up there. Neck and neck with a red shirted bay. They're striding together, up and down. Neither passing the other. The jockeys are hands and heels, with whips flying occasionally. No other horse is close but it's M and something else. M and something else. They dive at the post and I don't know.

"I think Moonstone Madness has got there," the race caller announces across the ground but still I'm holding my breath. Still Josh is stretched against me, his hand tight on my shoulder. Audrey is poised, waiting. We're all waiting while the caller rattles off the rest of the horses.

"Yes," he says, "Moonstone Madness by a nose to—"

I don't care who came second. I squeal. Audrey squeals.

I spin around to Josh and we're hugging, wrapped together as if we're lovers. And then for just a second our gazes meet, lock, and I sink against his lips. They catch me, cushion me, and caress me like silk. His mouth opens slightly against mine and our breaths intermingle. His hands clasp to my waist while mine find their way around his neck, my fingers threading through the silken curls peaking from his cap.

Our kiss is sweet and soft, in complete contrast to the excitement and chaos racing through me. Our mouths part and my squeal continues as if it hadn't stopped.

"She won," Josh says, as if he's astounded. Audrey hugs me, hugs him, hugs me again. Then Josh repeats himself before giving a head shake. He clasps my hand. "We have to go get her."

I shake my head. "No we. It's you. You get her, Josh."

"We." His hand holds mine securely and he takes me into the mounting yard where we greet M. She's blowing hard, sweated up, and the most beautiful sight in the world. Josh clips the lead on and together we walk her into the area for the winner.

Everything happens and I'm there for the ride. I won a horse in a raffle, kissed a man, and won a horse race. Today cannot get any better.

And then there's a trophy and a winner's cheque, so maybe it can get better.

I'm in a happiness bubble that I know must burst, but for now, I want to soar in this fragile state, enjoying every second of the dream. People congratulate me when Josh deserves all the congratulations and credit, but he's with M and I'm left here to soak up the accolades.

Eventually I make my way to the horse stalls, Audrey with me, and find Josh with a wet and thirsty M. He's holding a bucket while she slurps water. I walk close and slide my hand down M's neck. Josh's hand skims against mine.

"Thank you, M. Thanks, Josh." I hand him the cheque but he won't take it.

"That's yours."

"No way. You've done everything, and I won a raffle. I don't get the prize money. I won already." I shove the cheque into his back pocket, which isn't the best idea I've ever had. He jumps, M jumps and I run to Audrey.

"Classy," Audrey whispers. "Buns are good though?" I smack her arm.

Gingerly I walk back to Josh. "Sorry, I scared her again."

He grins. "I think I scared her, you just shocked me."

"Why? Girls don't stick their phone number in your pocket every day?" I bat my eyelids, clearly making it a joke.

"If that's your phone number, I'll take it. I'd like to see you again, Kat."

My eyes narrow. He can't mean as a date, can he? "For the races?"

"No, for you."

"But I'm..." I'm lost for words.

"Taken?" he asks.

"No. Not at all. Just a lousy friend, ask Audrey."

Audrey comes up. "We've been friends for twenty-three years, there's nothing lousy about you." She looks at Josh. "She's high maintenance, a little scatty, highly excitable, but a very dependable friend. I'll vouch for her."

He smiles at Audrey and then grins at me. "I work with that every day, you'll be a breeze. So, may I see you again?"

I nod, too excited to think of words. I fish in his back pocket again and drag out the envelope with the winner's cheque. I snag a pen from Audrey, and write my phone number down, mobile and landline and work. Then I write my address. Then I add my name to the top with a big smiley face. I fold the envelope and slip it back into his pocket.

"I'd love to see you again, Josh." I lean forward and plant a kiss on his cheek.

His hand slips around my waist and squeezes. "Talk to you soon, Kat."

Audrey leads me away. How? I've no idea. If it was up to me, I'd stand staring at those blue eyes forever. When we walk away, Moonstone Madness snickers softly and I hear Josh say, "Don't worry girl, we'll see her real soon."

Today got even better.

The End

Thank you for reading these stories. I hope you enjoyed them.

ABOUT THE AUTHOR

Catherine Evans is a city-born throwback to country genes. After completing an environmental biology degree, she desperately needed to move to the country. A job in agriculture was the perfect escape. After spending eighteen years in agricultural research and gaining a Masters degree in Agriculture, Cath has a passion for rural life.

Now living on the south coast of NSW, a large part of her heart belongs across the mountain ranges in the red dust.

If you want to know more, please visit Catherine's website www.catherineevansauthor.com

Catherine can be contacted by
mailto:catherine@catherineevansauthor.com

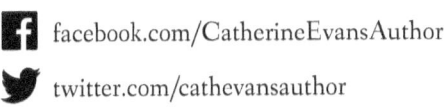

facebook.com/CatherineEvansAuthor

twitter.com/cathevansauthor

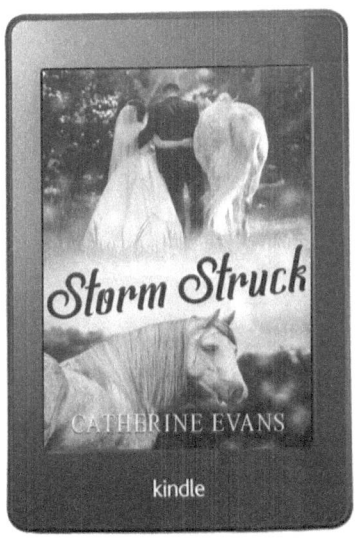